Logan

Illustrated by Robin LeDrew

By Margriet Ruurs

A Hodgepog Book

i

All characters in this story are fictitious.

Hodgepog Books gratefully acknowledges the ongoing support of the Canada Council for the Arts

Editors for Press:
Luanne Armstrong, Dorothy Woodend, Amanda Gibbs

Cover design by Dorothy Woodend
Inside layout by Dorothy Woodend
Set in Palatino and Helvetica in Quark XPress 4.1
Printed at Hignell Press

A Hodgepog Book for Kids
Published in Canada by Hodgepog Books
3476 Tupper Street
Vancouver, British Columbia V5Z 3B7
Phone: (604) 879-3079 Fax: (604) 681-1431
Email: dorothy@axion.net

Canadian Cataloguing in Publishing Data

Ruurs, Margriet, 1952-
  Logan's Lake

ISBN 0-9686899-8-1
I. Robin LeDrew, 1979- II. Title

PS8585.U97L63 2001   jC813'.54   C2001-911193-2
PZ7.R94Lo 2001

The Canada Council | Le Conseil des Arts
for the Arts | du Canada

To John and Joyce

Table of Contents

Chapter One: The Lake   Page 1

Chapter Two: Strangers   Page 6

Chapter Three: Reason to Worry   Page 15

Chapter Four: The Campaign   Page 20

Chapter Five: The Meeting   Page 26

Appendix   Page 41

Chapter One
The Lake

"Ka-ka-ka!"

Logan looks up to the waving tops of the trees where a shiny black raven calls out "Ka-ka!"

Logan smiles, "Ka-ka to you, too!" The raven chuckles.

Logan wanders down the path to the edge of the slushy lake. Winter has gathered wet leaves and sticks on the beach. He picks up a stick and tosses it onto the ice. Most of the lake is still frozen but there is a little edge of water at the beach now. The murky water looks like a slushy drink you can buy at the grocery store in town. Logan grins. He pictures the sign in the store, "Today's special: Mud Slushy".

Every day, the May sun warms the water a little more and melts the ice back further. Logan listens to the raven, now ka-ka-ing in the distance, teasing some whiskey jacks. He shades his eyes with one hand and stares off across the glistening lake until he spots what he was searching for. There they are, way off, where the frozen surface has opened up. Logan spots a flock of Canada geese, enjoying the northern sunshine just like he is.

That morning, when he was doing his schoolwork, he had heard the geese honking in the sky. He'd run outside, his mom and dad, too, just in time to see the "V" of geese circle above the lake, then come down to spend the day.

His dad had explained why geese always fly in a V formation. "They travel very far each year, going south when the snow comes, because in the south there is food and water throughout the winter. They come north again to the Yukon when winter is over, to lay their eggs and have their young. Some will stay on our lake here but others travel even further north, to the edge of the Arctic Ocean. They fly in a "V" because it makes the trip easier. The first goose, the leader, leads the way through the wind to help the ones that follow behind. They all take turns being the leader and flying together is much easier than trying such a long trip alone."

"Did you know," Logan's mom had added, "that when one goose gets sick or wounded, two other geese stay with him until he can fly again? Isn't that amazing!"

"The best part is that when the geese come back, winter is over!" Logan had said, "Now it really is spring! I like geese!"

And yet, even as he stands there on the beach, seeing the reassuring sign of returning geese, Logan senses something in the air. Something that makes him uneasy. He wishes he had brought his dog Kaya along, but she'd stayed behind with his dad. Logan turns his head and listens. Something is about to change, but he doesn't know what it is. He sighs and listens again. He hears the distant hammering of a woodpecker, the soft lapping of the lake. Logan takes a deep breath, smelling the pungent wet leaves that are visible again where the snow has melted.

Logan likes the sounds and smells of spring after the silence of winter. Winter at the lake is good, too. It is always cozy with the three of them in their log home. Dad chops lots of firewood in the fall so that the crackling wood stove keeps them warm all winter, even if it is fifty below outside! Logan likes the smell of soup bubbling on the stove as he does his school work at the kitchen table, Kaya lying at his feet. At night, they often play games or get lost in a good book. Logan likes to read everything: adventure stories, fantasy books and stories about far away countries. Books take him to places he's never been before. His dad sometimes challenges him to a game of Scrabble or Mindtrap. When his mom makes hot chocolate and they sit sipping it by the wood stove, Logan sometimes thinks he might like winter even better than summer.

Most of all Logan likes to stand out on the porch on a frosty winter night to watch the Northern Lights dance over the lake. Sometimes they are just a white light floating like a thin cloud in the sky. Other times the lights glow in green and orange, dancing and swirling like a colourful dust storm. Logan thinks he can hear the Northern Lights crackle while they dance.

Native people tell many wonderful legends about the Lights. Logan once went to the Storytellers

Festival in Whitehorse. He heard stories there about the Northern Lights. Some legends say that the lights are the ghosts of dead people, playing soccer in the sky! Another story told how the light resembles flowing robes of dancing ladies.

Logan likes to make up his own stories while he stands and watches the lights swirl across the sky. "It looks like dust," he thinks. "Maybe the angels are making their beds!" He watches until the inside of his nose is frozen and it gets hard to breathe. Then he dashes inside to warm up by the wood stove.

But spring is even better. Spring—when the geese come back bringing the sounds of new life with them. Logan listens to the cheerful chatter of cedar waxwings, the raw calling of ravens, the creaking of branches and the happy laughter of a squirrel. And yet, somewhere in the pit of his stomach, Logan knows that something is about to happen.

Chapter Two
Strangers

The forest around their log home is pretty quiet. Logan and his parents live out of town. It is more than an hour's drive to Whitehorse, the biggest city in the Yukon Territory. Logan's parents decided they didn't want him spending so much time on a school bus. Both of them are writers and they work from their home.

And so Logan doesn't go to public school. He does his school work at home. His dad has built him a desk and a bookcase of his own. Each morning Logan takes out his books and papers. His teacher from correspondence school lives far away. They have to mail his school work to the teacher and when it comes back in the mail it has lots of notes and stickers, a new pencil or stamps from the teacher. Sometimes Logan has to talk on a tape so that his teacher can hear how he reads a chapter of a new book or a poem.

Logan likes doing his school work. He doesn't mind math or science. He likes reading stories and books, but best of all he likes to write his own stories. He writes about the things around him. He's made up stories about his dog Kaya, stories in which Kaya rescues someone or digs up a buried treasure. Logan likes writing fictional stories because they let him use his own imagination. His teacher told Logan once that he was a very good writer. Dad had smiled. Hé writes articles for magazines for a living.

"Maybe you take after me!" he had said. Logan's mom writes books for kids about the environment and animals and other countries. "I'm sure he got it from me!" she had laughed.

Once in a while Logan wishes that he could go to a regular school and have friends to play with. But the good part about doing school work at home is that when he is finished, he can go outside to play on the beach and roam through the forest.

That's exactly what he's doing today. After he finished his school work, and after he heard the geese calling, he'd come out here to the beach.

He has a tree fort, too. Not far from the house. It's a place that is his alone; no one else ever goes there. But today Logan doesn't go to his tree fort. He

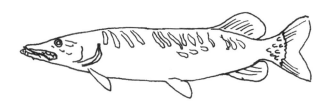

walks along the beach. Restless, he skips a stone across the frozen lake. It makes a hollow sound. "Maybe I woke up a trout!" he thinks.

In the summer he often fishes on the lake from his little boat. The very first time he ever fished, he caught a huge northern pike! Logan doesn't really remember but his dad likes to tell that story over and over. "We were just pushing off and already you had your hook overboard. I was rowing away from shore when the hook got stuck! I was just about to get mad at you for throwing your line overboard already and getting stuck in the weeds, when I saw that you weren't stuck at all. You had a big, fat pike on your line."

Logan knows that, even now, under the ice, the pike and trout are waiting for summer, just like he is. He wonders if they hear the honking of the geese, too.

Suddenly, Logan is startled out of his daydreaming by voices. Logan looks up. Not many people come here. The highway runs south of town but is still quite a distance from their house. Besides Logan's own house there are only two little cabins on the lake. Most people who come to this area are friends but Logan doesn't know the people he now spots. A little ways down, three men are walking on the beach. They point towards the lake. Their voices are carried on the wind. They turn and point at the trees. One man moves his arm as if he is sweeping away the forest. They laugh. "Yes," he hears one man say, "It's perfect."

The sight of the strange men makes Logan feel nervous. They seem so out of place in their business suits, with briefcases, on the beach. He doesn't know who they are or what they are doing there. Quick as a deer he darts down the trail, back to the house.

"Mom! Dad!"

"Whoa! What's up, guy?" His dad is standing on the porch.

Logan is out of breath. "I dunno, Dad," he pants, "but there are some men on the beach! I've never seen them before. They were talking about the lake and the trees. And…I didn't like it, Dad."

Dad frowns. "So, maybe it's true then," he says softly and stares off in the distance.

"What, Dad? What is true?" Logan follows his

dad into the house.

Dad sits down, leaning his head on his hands. Mom fills up his coffee mug. She looks worried, too.

"Last time we were in town," she says to Logan, "there were rumours. People said that a man from Outside was planning some development for the lake."

"What kind of development?" Logan asks.

"I think he wants to do something with the lake, build a boat launch. There are plans for a big hotel. A resort, I guess."

"Yes," Dad adds, "I've heard that they want to build a resort, with cabins, a restaurant, a boat launch and all that. For people to come up north and spend the summers on the lake."

"But I don't want a resort here!" Logan cries, "This is our lake. They can't just do that! I don't want lots of people coming here! They'd have to cut down trees and the raven lives there, and the moose."

"I know," his mom sighs and ruffles his hair, "but a resort would bring tourists and tourists would mean more jobs and more money. Some people will say that it would be good for the local economy."

"But we don't need it! Why do we need more money anyway? I don't want motorboats on the lake, they smell bad. And they'd scare the geese," Logan scoffs.

"The geese. Yeah." Dad runs a hand through his hair, making it stand up funny. He walks over to his desk and flips through some papers. He scratches his head and paces the floor. Logan knows his dad always does that when he is thinking hard. "But maybe we can do something. We don't just have to sit back and wait to see what will happen. If we wait, it might be too late to do anything. If we talk to the developer now, maybe we can make sure that they think about the environment before they start anything."

"There should be government agencies that can help. The lake needs protection" Mom adds.

They do a lot of talking that night. They talk about the resort and how it might affect their quiet life on the lake. Logan tries to imagine what it would be like, how it would change things. When he goes off to bed that night, Dad says, "Don't worry, Logan, we'll go and find out what the developer wants. And we'll make sure that the raven and the moose can stay here, too."

Logan is relieved. Doing something will be better than just waiting.

"Good," he says, "I just want to make sure that the animals won't have to leave and that the forest will be okay." His dad smiles, "You can do it, Logan. Your mom and I didn't name you Logan for nothing, you know. It is the name of Canada's tallest mountain! And the man it was named for, William Logan, was the first to survey all of Canada and make maps of the land. He did something worthwhile and that's why his name still lives on. You can do the same, and, if you really need to, you can move mountains!" Logan smiles. He falls asleep thinking of his favourite place in the world, their home on the lake.

Chapter Three
Reason to Worry

The next day, Logan and his dad go to town in the pick-up truck. They drive to the building where the developer has an office. When Logan sees the busy office with ringing telephones and huge maps on the walls, he gets that uneasy feeling in the pit of his stomach again. But the man who greets them seems nice enough. Logan recognizes him as one of the men from the beach. He introduces himself as Mr. Nicholson, shakes hands with Logan's dad and says that he'd be glad to explain the plans to him. The first thing Logan's dad wants to know is who owns the land that the development would be on. "Well, the town owns it," explains Mr. Nicholson, "and I will be leasing it." At first Mr. Nicholson just talks to Dad. He almost acts as if Logan isn't there. He talks about rezoning and bylaws. He also talks about the hotel, tells them how many rooms there will be, about the marina, the dock and how many boats he wants to rent out. He tells them about the view from the balconies and the possibility of a pool.

"But," says Logan all of a sudden, "what about outside? What about the animals that live where the hotel will be?"

"Animals?!" Mr. Nicholson looks at Logan as if he expects to see some animal crawling on the floor.

"Yeah, there's a moose living in the forest now, and deer, and lots of geese on the lake."

"Oh, those kind of animals, yes," he sounds relieved. "Well…uh…of course we are studying the natural environment. We will be looking at the impact of our development on the ecosystem."

"I would like to see your environmental impact

studies," Dad says, "and your sewage treatment plans."

"Oh." Mr. Nicholson scratches his head and nods slowly. Suddenly he doesn't seem as friendly any more.

"Will the animals be able to stay?" Logan wants to know.

"I…uh…I can't comment on that until the environmental impact study is completed," says Mr. Nicholson, trying to sound very important. It isn't long after that that Dad gets up. He thanks Mr. Nicholson and they leave. Logan can tell that his dad is not pleased. Logan himself has that same, restless feeling he had yesterday, on the beach.

Later, when they are home again, Logan thinks about what Mr. Nicholson said. He didn't really understand everything very well. "Mr. Nicholson said that they would study nature," he says to Dad, "but nature is here and he is there, in his office. How will he do that? What will he do?"

"Well," explains Logan's dad, "I think that Mr. Nicholson doesn't really know much about nature and how it can help him. He lives in a city. He's just come up North for this project, and he probably doesn't realize how good it is to be in nature, out by the lake. Maybe he's never really seen a moose or the geese."

Logan smiles. Slowly, an idea is taking shape inside his head!

"If people come here on their holidays, to get away from the city, then they will want to see nature, right? They will want to see animals and birds. So, if Mr. Nicholson builds this resort, he should make sure that he doesn't scare all the animals away."

"All right, Logan-my-man," Dad smiles, patting Logan on the shoulder, "now you're talking! And I don't know of a better person to tell Mr. Nicholson about the animals than you!"

"Me?" Logan looks worried at first. But then he smiles, "I guess I can tell him and I could show him." He is quiet for a while, thinking about what he could say to Mr. Nicholson. Then he sighs "What about the garbage that a resort like that would produce? What about those sewage plans you were talking about?

"We will look into that," his dad promises. "We will get in touch with all the government and environmental agencies who look after this sort of thing."

Logan wonders how he can help the animals and show Mr. Nicholson their importance at the same time. Dad has explained that they will have to talk to lots of people, to Town Council and many others to make them aware of how important the lake is to the animals. If they wait, and all the plans are approved, it would be too late to make any changes. Logan is starting to make notes in his binder. They include bits and pieces about where the moose lives and what they eat. About the geese and how they always come back after the winter. He makes notes about that pike he caught and then does a lot of reading about the salmon and the rainbow trout and all the other fish that live in the lake.

Chapter Four
The Campaign

Logan decides to write a letter to the Mayor:

Dear Mayor,

I live by the lake and see lots of animals every day. The moose lives here with her baby and lots of geese, too.
Now Mr. Nicholson wants to build a hotel by the lake. I am worried that it will make too much noise and garbage. I think that it will scare away the geese.
We have to make sure that enough trees will stay.
Please help us protect the forest and the lake.

Thank you,
Logan

Logan even writes a letter like that to the Minister of the Environment. His mom helps him to find the address. He decides to make posters, too, to put up in town to make more people aware of what is happening. Using his markers, he makes bright, large posters with a picture of the geese, and some with a moose.

Help save our wildlife by the lake!
Find out what kind of development is happening!
We need jobs but wildlife, too!

On their next trip into town, he takes the posters and puts them up in the supermarket, the post office and on the bulletin board of the Library.

They are very busy during the next few weeks. Logan's dad talks to Mr. Nicholson several times. He makes lots of phone calls and types away at the computer. He sends many big envelopes to magazines with stories about the raven, the eagles, the moose with her calf. He sends them photos of the black bear on the beach, of the wildflowers in the summer, and articles about the migration of the geese.

Logan does his school work in the mornings. He tries to learn more about the animals around him so that he can tell Mr. Nicholson about them. In the books he borrows from the library, he reads about the salmon and discovers that salmon are born on the bottom of the creeks coming into the lake. They hatch from tiny eggs that are laid amongst the rocks and gravel. The salmon spend their first year in the lake, as tiny little fish called fry. They feed in the lake until they grow into fingerlings! Then they leave the lake, following the creeks, streams and rivers all the

23

way down to the ocean.

"Get this, Dad," Logan tells his dad, "they spend three years, three years, in the ocean, swimming all over the place and then they come back to the exact same creek they were born! I wonder how they know where that was. They swim all the way back up the same rivers and streams to this lake! And then they lay their own eggs and they die." Logan can't get over what a miracle it is that those salmon know how to do that.

After Logan finishes his schoolwork, he goes outside and enjoys the beach and the woods. One afternoon, his mom calls him from the porch. "Come, quickly!" she says in a hushed voice. When Logan gets to the porch she points towards the scrawny pine tree in front of the house. She hung a hummingbird feeder in one of its branches a few days ago. Smiling, she points at the feeder. A buzzing little bird is sipping from it! Logan grins. His mom whispers "They came back, too! Isn't it amazing!"

Logan remembers that last year his mom had told him about this incredible trip the tiny hummingbirds make. "How far did they come?" he asks.

"Well, they spend the winter in southern Mexico," his mom replies, "They fly about 5000 kilometres to get back here during the summer! And look at those tiny wings!"

The birds hover so fast that Logan can't really see any wings at all, just a blur. "They beat their wings about 200 times per second!" his mom smiles.

They admire the little summer visitors for a while and then go back inside. Mom is busy, too. She's on the phone a lot, talking to people about the environment that needs to be protected. "The animals can't do it," she smiles, "so we have to speak up for them."

Logan laughs. He can just imagine the animals doing it themselves. Would the moose have a meeting? And the raven fly around with a banner that says 'Don't Cut My Trees Down!'

Chapter Five
The Meeting

Logan often drives into town with his mom or dad now. They talk to different people in offices. One day they even have to talk on the radio. Logan and his dad sit in the studio, a small room with windows all around and a red light over the door. It is very quiet in the room. They put headphones on and have a microphone in front of them. When the radio announcer starts talking with them, Logan is very nervous. His stomach hurts and his hands are sweaty. But soon they talk about the lake and the beach, about what Logan sees there every day. And he forgets about how many people might be listening to him right now. Some people phone in with questions about the lake, the animals and the development. Some of them sound mad. They want a big development and don't care much about its impact. That scares Logan. He asks his dad about it, after the radio show.

Dad says it's okay. "Everybody has the right to have an opinion," he says, "Some people think a resort would be good for our town and they don't think about the consequences it may have for the environment."

Logan's dad reads the newspaper every night and he starts showing Logan the section called 'Letters to the Editor'. Pretty soon Logan scans the newspaper every day to read other people's opinions. There are letters from people who really want a resort because they are out of work and construction will bring money to town. There are also letters from people who are fighting the development and agree with Logan that the lake needs to be protected. Sometimes, after reading several letters, Logan isn't sure what to think anymore! Then he just goes out for a walk along the beach until the wind clears his thoughts while the raven chuckles at him from the tree branches.

One day, someone from town hall calls to tell them that a meeting has been set up by Town Council. Mr. Nicholson will be there to explain his plans. They ask Logan's dad to be there, too, to talk about the natural environment and how he thinks a resort would affect the lake and the forest. Logan and his parents are excited on the night of the meeting. Because lots of people are expected, the meeting is to take place at the school. As they follow the crowd into the school gym, Logan is happy to see that so many people have come. Chairs have been set up in the gym and there is a podium with a microphone up front. The Mayor and the members of Town Council are all sitting behind a table in front of the audience. A lady from the newspaper takes pictures. Logan even sees a television crew.

Mr. Nicholson is there, too, in his dark business suit. He is one of the first speakers. He tells the people about the resort that he wants to build, how big it will be and how many tourists will come.

29

He has put up maps and charts with drawings of the resort. It looks pretty attractive. He tells them how much money the tourists will spend in town and how, because of the resort, many people will get jobs. Logan sighs. It sounds like a good plan. He is starting to understand what a difficult problem this is! Maybe it would be good to build a huge hotel and a bar and a pool, a boat dock. But then he thinks of the quiet wilderness, of how the animals need the lake and the trees. No! He squeezes his hands into fists. No, no matter how nice it sounds, the animals and the trees have rights, too! They should be thinking of them first!

Mr. Nicholson goes on and on, about roads that will be paved to make the lake more accessible, and about the marina that he wants to build.

When he is done, the people clap politely. Logan's stomach feels tight. Will everybody agree with the man? He tries to think of the lake. Squeezing his eyes shut tight he pictures the waving tree tops. He can almost feel the breeze as it comes off the lake and stirs his hair. And suddenly, as if the vision gives him courage, Logan knows what he has to do.

Mr. Nicholson has finished his talk. The people cough and shuffle their feet. They talk softly amongst themselves. Slowly, Logan gets up from his seat. Heart racing, he stuffs his sweaty fists into his pockets. His knees feel sort of funny and, when he gets to the microphone, he hopes that his voice will be there when he starts to talk. He takes a deep breath.

"I…um…I have never done this," he starts shakily, amazed to hear his own voice echoing through the gym, "but I want to tell you about the lake."

The people look at him expectantly. Some elbow each other. Someone giggles because a kid wants to say something. Logan has to force himself to think of the animals, not of all these people staring at him. Then he starts talking. He tells them, too fast at first, about the geese and why they come to the lake, how they fly in V's and help each other to make their enormous trip every year.

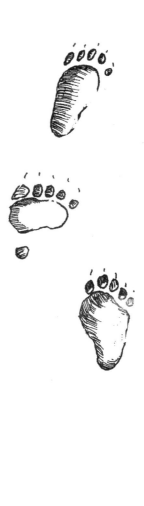

31

He sees someone nod in agreement and that makes him feel more confident. His rapidly beating heart seems to slow down a bit as he helps the audience to remember fishing trips they all have taken, without a resort at the lake. He tells them about the salmon and the pike that live in the lake, about the moose that had a baby last spring, and how many pounds of leaves and twigs she eats each day.

"Maybe, when people come that will stay in the hotel and the cabins, they would like to see and do all these things, too. But if the trees are gone, all the animals will be gone, too. Then the tourists won't enjoy it as much. I think, if you want to have boats on the lake, that you should try to find boats that don't make noise or pollute the lake so the geese and the fish will stay. If you just build a big building and all those things, it will be just like in a city…and that's not why people would come here. Maybe the resort shouldn't be so big…Maybe you should plan trails for people to hike so they might meet the moose!"

Some people mumble in agreement. That's all Logan has to say. He steps off the stage, afraid. But then he hears them clap. They must have liked what he said because they clap loudly. Much more loudly than after Mr. Nicholson spoke. Some people even cheer.

Logan lets out a deep breath. He feels like a

balloon that has all the air let out. He quickly slips back in his chair, next to his mom and dad. His dad squeezes his hand real hard and his mom claps him on the shoulder. They look proud of Logan.

After the meeting, the Mayor comes over to them. She shakes hands with Logan's dad and then she shakes hands with Logan. "Well spoken, young man," she smiles as she moves on to speak with other people.

Mr. Nicholson comes over, too. He looks at Logan as if he sees him for the first time. "Well, well, young man, I was very impressed with what you said there!" he says. "In fact, after what you said, I would like to ask you to show me around the lake and tell me what you know. Will you do that?"

"Sure," Logan agrees. Maybe that is the way he can really help.

Two days later, Mr. Nicholson

comes by the house. Logan is standing on the porch when Mr. Nicholson drives up in his shiny, black car. Logan hops down and shows Mr. Nicholson the trail to the beach. A hummingbird buzzes away. Together they walk through the woods, looking around, listening.

"These are aspen trees," Logan says, "not birch, like most people think. And that tall one is a lodge pole pine. Do you know why it's called lodge pole pine?"

Mr. Nicholson shakes his head, "No. Why?"

"Native people used them for the centre pole when they were building their lodge." Logan strokes the rough bark as if greeting an old friend.

"There," he whispers suddenly, grabbing the sleeve of Mr. Nicholson's jacket, "there is the woodpecker." And he points at the black-and-white bird, clinging to the bark of a tree, beating a rapid greeting.

"You sure have good eyes!" Mr. Nicholson laughs.

Logan tells him about the moose and shows him where she ate leaves off the branches. He shows him where a porcupine nibbled on bark and the leftovers of a squirrel's pine cone dinner. He points out musty smelling mushrooms, leftovers from last fall, and blossoms that will soon turn to berries.

"These are soap berries," he says. "They're called soap berries because native people used them to wash clothes!" He points out the high bush cranberries and they even find the paw print of a black bear in the soft clay along the trail.

When they reach the beach, Logan points to where the geese stay overnight. He tells Mr. Nicholson the story of how he caught his first pike. They look at the waving tops of the tall trees and talk about how long it takes, up North, for a tree to grow that tall, standing up to cold and wind.

By the time Mr. Nicholson leaves, Logan feels that he's made a friend. A hesitant friend perhaps but one who now knows how important the animals are to the people, and how important the trees are to the animals. All Logan can do now is wait, and hope that he has helped.

Later that week, Logan receives an impressive looking letter addressed to him. The envelope has a red and gold emblem on it. He tears it open hastily. Inside is a letter on very official looking paper from the Minister of the Environment. The letter says that he is studying the problem and that he will be in touch with the Mayor and Town Council. He thanks Logan for his concern and says that he is sure the right decision will be made. Logan isn't sure if that is good news or not. The letter really doesn't have a lot

of information.

Logan finds it hard to concentrate on his school work now. His thoughts flutter out of the window to be with the raven, when he has to do math. After his school work, Logan wanders down the path between the trees towards the lake. He sits on his haunches to watch a toad jumpity-jump over some twigs. A woodpecker beats a rapid 'ttttrrrrrr' on the bark of a tree. And a squirrel rushes up the tree trunk, then sits on a branch scolding Logan.

Logan tries to imagine what it would be like if there was a huge resort just down the beach. He would see different things than he sees now. He'd see people and lawn chairs and a large building. He would hear different sounds than he hears now. He would hear radios and voices.

It would even smell differently than it smells now. He would smells cars and motorboats. He takes a deep breath and smells pungent pine and wet moss.

Suddenly, Logan hears his dad's voice. "Logan! Logan!" He jumps up and runs towards the house. Mr. Nicholson's car is parked on the path and they're all standing on the porch.

"Hi Logan," Mr. Nicholson says," I came to tell you something you might like!" He smiles and unrolls a big roll of white paper full of blue lines, drawings of buildings and maps. "We have completed our environmental impact study and we have talked to many people like you and your parents."

He pauses, and Logan, still panting, looks at him expectantly.

"I have decided," Mr. Nicholson continues, "to change the plans. I have cut down the size of the resort to almost half. We won't make it quite the resort I first had planned." He grins, "Someone showed me that a small wilderness lodge would be much more profitable up here!" He winks at Logan.

"There is too much opposition to motorboats on the lake. We'll restrict it to canoes and rowboats only. No noise. No pollution." He rubs his chin and looks out over the gently lapping waves at the shore. "I have talked to Town Council and they have agreed to rezone the land to allow a small resort. Just a lodge where people come to relax. Maybe we'll have an interpretive program so city people can learn to appreciate nature more. Like me," he adds with a chuckle.

"Does that mean that the forest will stay?" Logan wants to know.

"It means we will have to cut down some trees to build a lodge, and we'll make some more trails to the beach. But we will make sure that we disturb the forest and the animals as little as we can."

"Hurray!" Logan cries out loud. He turns around and, arms wide in the air, he yells "Hurray!" A squirrel scoots up a tree at the sound of Logan's voice, echoing around the lake. "It's okay, squirrel," Logan laughs, "you can stay. Your tree won't be cut down!"

Mr. Nicholson laughs. "And the geese can come back next spring as always," Dad sighs.

"Look," Logan points, "even the raven is celebrating!" The shiny black raven chuckles, high in a tree top.

"Ka-ka-ka!" he calls, looking over his woods.

"You're welcome!" Logan laughs. They all

watch as a majestic bold eagle soars through the sky overhead, a kite without a string, sailing over the lake and forest like a promise. A promise to be kept forever.

Appendix

Logan lives in northern Canada in the Yukon Territory near the capital city of Whitehorse. The Yukon is a great place to see wildlife. Almost 60% of the Yukon is covered in forest. The boreal forest includes
- coniferous (with needles) trees: spruce, pine and fir;
- deciduous (with leaves) trees: poplar, birch, alder, aspen and willow.

Northern shrubs include blueberries, cranberries, soap berries and more.

The forests of the Yukon are home to many animals. The red fox, the weasel, ermine and red-tailed hawks live upon small prey like mice. Moose and snowshoe hare browse on the twigs and leaves of young trees. Black and grizzly bears live in the Yukon, and grey wolves and coyotes hunt throughout the north.

Yukon birds include thrushes, warblers, woodpeckers, chickadees and more. Eagles soar the northern skies while ptarmigan and grouse hide in the shrubs.

McClintock Bay near Whitehorse is a critical habitat for migrating waterfowl in spring. These include trumpeter swans, ducks and geese.

Northern Pike, lake trout, salmon and Arctic grayling are just some of the species that abound in northern lakes and rivers.

Beavers build their dams and lodges around lakes across the North.

To learn more about the Yukon's environment, Yukon Renewable Resources has great publications that will tell you about birds, mammals and forests in the North, including *Yukon's Wildlife Viewing Guide*.
Write to:
Renewable Resources
Government of the Yukon
Box 2703
Whitehorse, Yukon, Y1A 2C6
http://www.renres.gov.yk.ca

Ask for the booklet:
Reading Yukon Forests
from Yukon Conservation Society
302 Hawkins Street
Whitehorse, Yukon, Y1A 1X6

Canadian Wildlife Service, Environment Canada
Mile 917.6B Alaska Highway
Whitehorse, Yukon, Y1A 5X7

For environmental information elsewhere in Canada,
check out the Environment Canada website:
http://www.ec.gc.ca/envhome.html

The Canadian Wildlife Service has a great
information series you can ask for,
Hinterland Who's Who series (fact sheets on birds,
mammals and related topics):
Canadian Wildlife Service
Environment Canada
Ottawa, Ontario
K1A 0H3
Tel: (819) 997-1095
Fax: (819) 997-2756 (No publications will be faxed
back)
Email: cws-scf@ec.gc.ca

Margriet Ruurs has been writing children's and educational materials for a long time. Having been born and raised in the Netherlands, Margriet is bilingual. She writes and translates into Dutch and English. Margriet, her husband and two sons now live in British Columbia's Okanagan Valley where Margriet teaches writing programs in schools. She has a Master's Degree in Education from Simon Fraser University and she speaks at conferences around North America.

Robin LeDrew lives on a piece of land she has loved since she was thirteen. She listens to people for a living, drawing and writing when she gets a chance. Her illustrated fantasy, **A Future So Bright**, can be found in the Lumby Virtual Village at www.monashee.com

If you liked this book...
you might enjoy these other Hodgepog Books:

For grades 5–7

Written on the Wind
by Anne Dublin, illustrated by Avril Woodend
ISBN 1-9686899-5-7   Price $6.95

and for readers in grades 3–5,
or read them to younger kids

Ben and the Carrot Predicament
by Mar'ce Merrell, illustrated by Barbara Hartmann
ISBN 1-895836-54-9   Price $4.95

Getting Rid of Mr. Ributus
by Alison Lohans, illustrated by Barbara Hartmann
ISBN 1-895836-53-0   Price $6.95

A Real Farm Girl
by Susan Ioannou, illustrated by James Rozak
ISBN 1-895836-52-2   Price $6.95

A Gift for Johnny Know-It-All
by Mary Woodbury, illustrated by Barbara Hartmann
ISBN 1-895836-27-1   Price $5.95

Mill Creek Kids
by Colleen Heffernan, illustrated by Sonja Zacharias
ISBN 1-895836-40-9   Price $5.95

Arly & Spike
by Luanne Armstrong, illustrated by Chao Yu
ISBN 1-895836-37-9   Price $4.95

A Friend for Mr. Granville
by Gillian Richardson, illustrated by Claudette
Maclean
ISBN 1-895836-38-7   Price $5.95

Maggie & Shine
by Luanne Armstrong, illustrated by Dorothy Woodend
ISBN 1-895836-67-0   Price $6.95

Butterfly Gardens
by Judith Benson, illustrated by Lori McGregor
McCrae
ISBN 1-895836-71-9   Price $5.95

The Duet
by Brenda Silsbe, illustrated by Galan Akin
ISBN 0-9686899-1-4 $5.95

Jeremy's Christmas Wish
by Glen Huser, illustrated by Martin Rose
ISBN 0-9686899-2-2 $5.95

Let's Wrestle
by Lyle Weis, illustrated by Will Milner and Nat Morris
ISBN 0-9686899-4-9 $5.95

A Pocketful of Rocks
by Deb Loughead
ISBN 0-9686899-7-3 $5.95

Sebastian's Collection Connection
by Gwen Molnar, illustrated by Mia Hansen
ISBN 1-9686899-6-5   Price $5.95

and for readers in grade 1-2,
or to read to pre-schoolers

Sebastian's Promise
by Gwen Molnar, illustrated by Kendra McCleskey
ISBN 1-895836-65-4   Price $4.95

Summer With Sebastian
by Gwen Molnar, illustrated by Kendra McClesky
ISBN 1-895836-39-5   Price $4.95

The Noise in Grandma's Attic
by Judith Benson, illustrated by Shane Hill
ISBN 1-895836-55-7   Price $4.95

Pet Fair
by Deb Loughead, illustrated by Lisa Birke
ISBN 0-9686899-3-0 $5.95